Snort's Special Gift

This book belongs to:

_____

A gift from:

_____

ISBN: 978-1-59298-423-7

Library of Congress Control Number: 2011931255
Book design by Mayfly Design (mayflydesign.net)
Printed in the United States of America
Third Printing: 2017

20 19 18 17   6 5 4 3

Beaver's Pond Press, Inc.
7108 Ohms Lane
Edina, MN 55439-2129
(952) 829-8818
www.BeaversPondPress.com

To order, visit www.BeaversPondBooks.com
or call (800) 901-3480. Reseller discounts available.

To my angels: Sensei and Sushi
Thank you for your unconditional love.
Because of you, I wrote this book.
—Suzann Yue

For my mom Meifang Yang
—Lin Wang

"Mommy, Daddy, look!" Savy jumped up and down in the pile of leaves and laughed. "I found Snort's ball!" Savy threw it as far as she could. "Go get it, Snort!" she yelled.

Snort looked at the ball and put her head down. Savy's little brother Sunne ran after the ball instead.

Savy was worried. "Snort doesn't play fetch anymore!" she told her Mommy.

"Savy, Snort is sick." Mommy explained. "Your daddy and I need to talk to you and Sunne about Snort."

"Why?" Savy asked.

"Honey, Snort is in a lot of pain. Daddy and I feel it's time that we help Snort's aches and pains go away."

"How?" Savy asked.

"The veterinarian will give Snort special doggy medicine, I promise it won't hurt Snort. All her pain will go away, and she will go live in heaven," Daddy told her.

"I don't want Snort to go!" Savy cried.

"None of us do," Mommy replied.

"Who's going to play fetch with Snort?" Sunne asked.

"The angels will," Mommy explained. "They'll take good care of her."

"I'm going to miss Snort," Savy said sadly.

"We all will, but our memories of her will live forever in our hearts," Daddy explained.

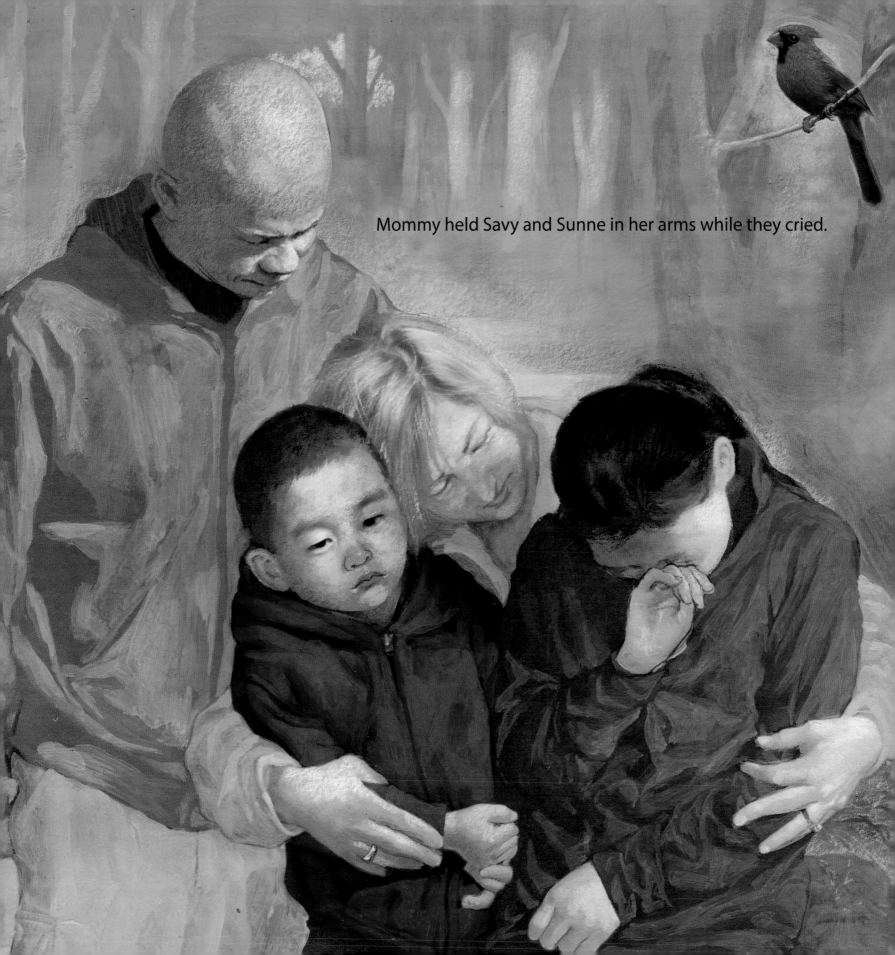

Mommy held Savy and Sunne in her arms while they cried.

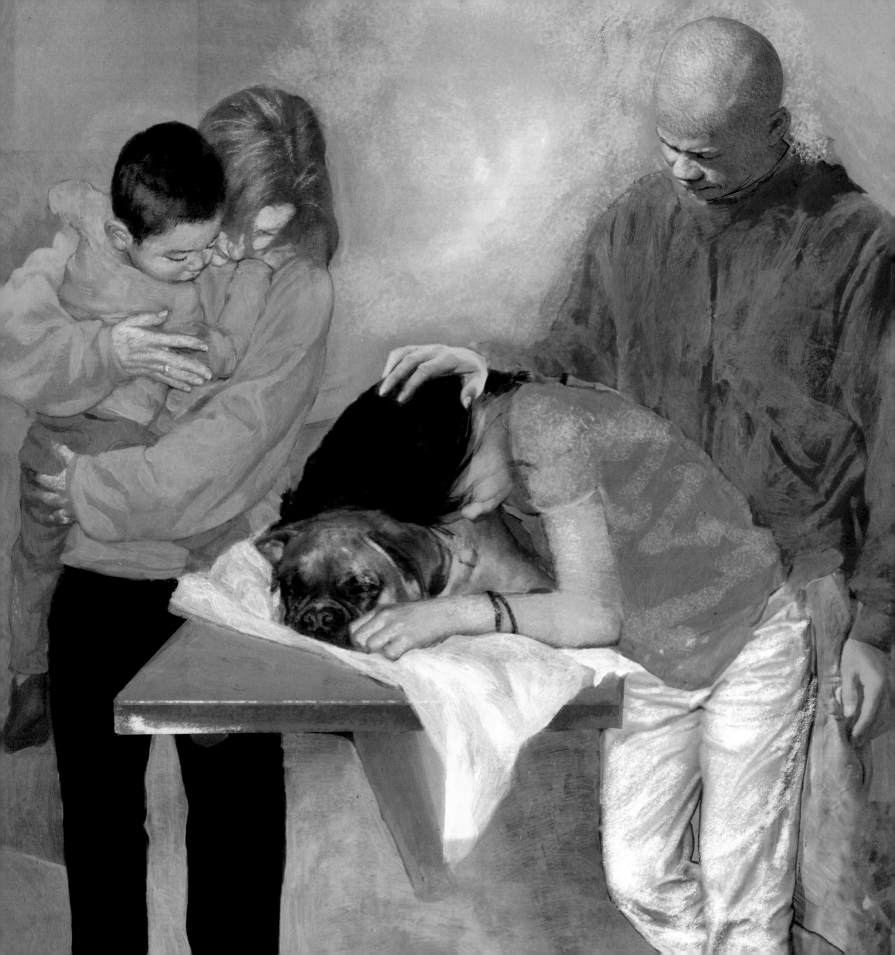

Several days after Snort went to heaven, Savy, Sunne, and Daddy were cleaning out the garage. All of them were feeling very sad.

"Hey, I have a great idea!" Daddy said. "Why don't we plant a tree in Snort's memory?"

"Cool! Can we get it today?" Savy asked.

"Please?" Sunne added, jumping up and down.

"We sure can! Go get Mommy!" Daddy answered.

They all jumped into the van, and off they went to the tree farm.

"Mommy, how about this tree?" asked Savy.

"Oh, that's a pretty tree," Mommy replied.

"It looks like a Christmas tree! If we get this tree, can we have Christmas every day?" Sunne asked.

Daddy laughed. "Not quite!"

"Can we decorate the tree for Snort every Christmas?" Savy asked.

"Sure! Snort loved Christmas!" Mommy laughed. "Remember how she chewed on the gingerbread ornaments every year?"

"She chewed all the bows off my presents, too!" Sunne said.

When they got home, everyone worked together to plant Snort's new tree.

Daddy dug the hole, and Mommy set the tree gently into the ground. Sunne helped push the dirt around the tree's roots. Savy made sure it had plenty of water so it would grow tall and strong.

The next day, Savy's teacher, Mrs. Andris, asked the class to write stories about someone special in their life.

Robert yelled out, "I'm going to write about my babysitter Sherry!"

Kay shouted, "My grandma is special! I'm writing about her!"

Savy sat quietly at her desk and thought hard.

That evening at dinner, Savy told her parents about her school project.

"Who are you going to write about?" Mommy asked.

"I'm going to write about Snort," Savy said.

"That's a great idea, Savy!" Daddy said. "Snort was your best friend!"

After dinner, Savy got her notebook.
She sat down outside by Snort's tree
and started to write her story.

The next day, Mrs. Andris asked, "Does anyone want to share their story with the class?" Savy slowly raised her hand.

Mrs. Andris smiled. "Great, Savy! Please read for us."

Savy was nervous, but she took a deep breath and began.

"Most of you probably wrote about people, but I wrote about my dog, Snort. I gave her this special name because she snored all night and kept me awake. Snort needed to go to heaven because she was very sick. I brought my favorite picture of us to share with the class."

"Snort was special to me because she taught me important things."

"Snort taught me patience. She would wait all day for my little brother and me to get home from school. She showed me how to be patient for something you want and love."

"Snort taught me to be safe. She never left our yard without the family. She reminded me never to wander off alone."

"Snort taught me how to be heard. She used her loud bark to scare strangers out of our yard. She showed me how to speak up and not be shy."

"Snort taught me loyalty. She followed me everywhere. She taught me to be helpful when my loved ones need me."

Savy's eyes filled with tears, and her voice trembled. "I miss Snort. But I know she's happy and playing fetch with the angels! I thank Snort for teaching me so much and being my best friend. I know she will always watch over me from heaven."

When Savy was done, the whole class stood up and clapped.
Savy proudly took a bow.

That Christmas, Savy received a wonderful gift. She found a lost puppy wandering around Snort's tree. Savy's family decided to give the puppy a home.

Savy knew that this sweet puppy was a gift from Snort. She named her puppy Angel. Savy felt lucky to have a new friend to help her decorate Snort's tree every Christmas. She knew that Angel would teach her special lessons too!

_____ Special Gift

I love you because…

You're a gift to me because…

_____

_____

_____

_____

You made me laugh when…

_____

_____

_____

You're my best friend because…

_____

_____

Attach pet photo
3½ x 5"

You taught me…

_____

_____

Best Friends